PUBLISHED AUTHOR AT 103
Never Too Old!

Stories and Musings of
Ken Heckerson

Kenneth Andrew Heckerson

PUBLISHED AUTHOR AT 103 - Never Too Old!
Stories and Musing of Ken Heckerson

Copyright © 2022 Kenneth Andrew Heckerson

ISBN: 9798847448079

The Butterfly

In the garden nearby
So much admired, butterfly
Flit and flutter by wide wings
With harmony and nature sings
Be reverent witness, with a sigh
Pray the faith, fills the sky
Welcome those angelic wings
Heaven sent by sovereign kings

By Ken Heckerson 2021

1

My Life, My Story - A Brief Summary

I was born on August 31, 1919 in England and came to American in 1920 through Ellis Island. I was fortunate to have come when I did. My family moved to St. Joseph, MO because we had family there. I lived there for a few years, but not many. I had four brothers; three older and one younger. My dad got a job in Chicago and when I was about five years old we moved there. That is where I grew up and where I finished high school.

My childhood was very typical. I don't know how to compare it with anything else. We did things that they don't do today. We would sit in a tree for days on end. We were mad about camping, fishing and all of those kinds of activities. We looked forward to going to northern Wisconsin to go fishing and I would say half the population of Chicago felt the same way. There were a lot of interesting things in Chicago. The world's fair was held in 1933 and Riverview Recreation Park was also there, with everything you could imagine. Every day I would wonder how I could get a ticket to go there. The city had a lot of wonderful things, but also had bad things too. We did some bad things that we could have been killed so many times. As kids, I think we thought we were bullet proof.

I was drafted into the Army in 1941. I was sent to California and then from there went to Fort Lewis, WA for boot camp. After that tour, I was sent to Northern California where I did a little more training. By that time, the Japanese dropped the bomb on Pearl Harbor. I was eventually assigned to the 40th Division. I was sent to Hawaii because they thought the Japanese would invade the islands, although they never did. I lived at Schofield Barracks, near Honolulu and I sat there for a year and a half and all we did was drink saké and watch the hula girls. Eventually I was shipped to the Solomon Islands in the South Pacific.

It was pretty obvious that we were going through a holding pattern until the Navy and the Air Force were completely organized to attack the Philippines, which were already occupied by the Japanese. We went through a variety of activities. One of islands I went to was Guadalcanal. We had opportunities to visit with the natives and they had nothing, not even clothing. I felt sorry for them.

We also went to New Britain, another island and then finally allies launched their attack on the Philippines. We went to Luzon with other Army elements. We captured Clark Field and the Zambales Mountains, opening the road for the 1st

Calvary to go down and capture Manila. There were a lot of nasty things; bad weather, disease, people getting killed. There were Japanese spies infiltrated into the Filipino population. You didn't know who was who and many people were killed. I imagine that was about the time of the Bataan March with allied prisoners.

There were a couple of active campaigns and I've written stories about some of it. Our company commander of the 1st Battalion, 160th Infantry Regiment, was about 30 feet away from me at one of the campaigns. I saw him laying on his back, he'd been shot. A fellow soldier, Lopez, crawled out under enemy machine gun fire and pulled the commander back to safety. Lopez was awarded the Silver Star and sent home. It was an act of chivalry. The command died of his wounds. I jumped behind a bombed out bulldozer or else I would have gotten it. Finally, they dropped the Atomic Bomb that was approved by President Truman and that changed everything. Bit by bit, some of us got to go home and I think some went to Korea.

There were good moments and bad moments. Overall, it was a pretty bad experience. We had launched a campaign in the Philippines and part of the time we were living in foxholes and not getting a very good diet, but that's war. War is nasty. One of our men stepped on a Japanese Personnel Mine and it shredded his legs. He laid there and died within a few minutes. All kinds of bad and rotten things happened. That's about all I can tell you.

That was the end of the active campaigns after we drove the Japanese out. | got back in 1945. When we got out at Fort Sheridan, Illinois, there was no one there to welcome us home - no one. There was a woman standing at the gate and wanted to know if I would like to get into a Vaudeville show in downtown Chicago. I said yeah. It was sponsored by State Street Clothiers and the show was with Olson & Johnson, it was titled Laughing Room Only. We danced with chorus girls on the stage. Ultimately, we received a full entire of free civilian clothing as we were still in uniform. It was a lot of fun. Then finally I went home.

It was time to start back with civilian life. I couldn't get a job. This was probably a residual condition as a result of the crash of the stock market in 1929. In other words, the economy was still in the recovery stage. I ended up getting a job in sales in California.

In the meantime, my folks separated. I took my mother with me and that is where she is buried. I sent my dad to live with a brother in Denver, so the family broke up. I lost my job in California and I could have gone to a related company in California so I could have continued similar kind of work, but I didn't do that. I went to Milwaukee where I had a brother and I lived there for about 35-40 years.

I was married for one year, around 1970. She was a nice girl and I liked her, but she convinced me right away that she didn't care for me at all. I was pretty discouraged, but I could see that it was not a good situation and not worth it. I got a divorce and I never got married again, nor did I have kids.

Around 2006, I moved to Prairie du Chen because I got tired of the noise and congestion in Milwaukee. I lived there for a year, but there was nothing there other than a Wal-Mart, not even a senior center.

I drove to La Crosse and decided it would be a better place to live. La Crosse is a pretty good town and has a wide variety of activities. It's a satisfying place for almost anybody and it has a nice atmosphere with bluffs and the river.

I've always been in touch with the VA, but not so much until I came to La Crosse. I never had a need for it. I have a medical policy, so I've been going to Mayo Skemp since I've been to La Crosse. I currently drive and live in my own home on French Island, but I have gone through the VA to maybe look at living at King in Waupaca. I don't really know exactly what I'm going to do, but l'd prefer to be here.

I had my 100th birthday party at the end of August 2019. I think almost 200 people came. I'm a member of the American Legion and a member of the Ukulele Club. I can't play a tune, but no one cares. I've learned that some of the members of these clubs are there for the same reason I am, sociability. We hold our meetings at the Moose Lodge, which is very active. Things like this helps you fill up life because I'm not a person that goes home and stares at the wall.

The secret to life cannot be answered in one sentence. I've decided to make a copy and pass it out to everyone at my party because I know they'll ask me why I'm living so long. It involves a variety of things. I have a variety of medical books that I read and the more I read them, the more interesting it gets. I read nutrition and know a lot about it.

You have to have a positive attitude and I think I do. I think there are more good things ahead of me and I turn my back to the bad stuff. You've got to face up to reality. I never did like the Army, but in the

Army, you learned discipline. There was a day when my doc told me that I had an ulcer caused by smoking. He told me I had to make a decision to stay healthy and get rid of the ulcer, but if I kept smoking I wouldn't be able to handle fried foods or whiskey. I decided right then that I'd rather have my Jack Daniels than my cigarettes and I quit in one day. Period. Discipline.

I laugh a lot, and laughing it gets tension out of your body and reduces stress on the heart. There ya have it and everyone I talk to winds up laughing. If you take life seriously, you're going to be disappointed.

The most important people in your life are your intimate friends and your family. You should be well aware of that in terms of your relationships. People with bad habits, forget them and walk away.

I have about four hobbies. I make my own bread and soup, I do photography and I'm also a graphologist, which is handwriting analysis. I can look at someone's handwriting and tell you all about them even if I have not met them. It's a lot of fun, but I have to be careful about what I say because I could be wrong; comments really have to be conservative. I've been doing this off and on for years as a hobby.

We should respect all human life; who they are and where they come from. I've had my fair share of unhappy experiences. I feel that I have a few good things ahead and I'm going to try and appreciate all of it.

***

Update: At the age of 101 I quit driving and moved out of my home and into a nursing home in La Crosse. On August 31, 2022 I celebrate my 103rd birthday!

2

My Michelangelo

My participation in the recent Freedom Honor Flight of September 18, 2010 to Washington, DC., was rewarding and fulfilling. I met currently active young military men, volunteers, co-workers and various members of the flight team.

With respect to my previous story about the flight, there is some repletion here that I found difficult to avoid. My focus in this communication is more about the patriotic response toward the Vets, rather than the flight its self. Importantly it seemed obvious that all members supporting the flight had recognition of fallen soldiers in earlier campaigns. Later when I was queried about the flight I said, "I cannot answer it in one sentence," so I wrote a story about it. This might be termed, 'the rest of the story'.

The treatment of the Vets was overwhelming from the prep activity before take-off at Hangar #4, all through the flight. When we returned at 11:30 PM that night, the same demonstrative crowd welcomed us with great ovation. Seeing all the memorials at Washington, DC was a unique and heartwarming experience. Visiting there is to know the history of the country and is best represented there.

During the return flight, an announcement was made that we had received mail. I questioned this since we were in the air. But I was handed a large envelope with my name on it. The content was 'well wishing, Bon Voyage' cards from the young students at Summit elementary School on French Island, La Crosse, WI. Earlier in the day we received a bag of items and similar cards from the children at St. Patrick's School in Onalaska, WI and Northwoods International School in La Crosse, WI.

They were simple and direct cards of good will and well wishes, directed to the Vets of WW2. In essence the statements had strong impact such as: *thanks for saving our country, thank you for your courage in the war, thank you for saving our freedom.*

Feelings of sincerity and admiration were inscribed in all of the cards. As a result of these superlative messages, I felt a need to respond and say, "Thank You" in like manner. I thought a rejoinder would be appropriate, that the vets didn't take the cards for granted and the cards indeed represented an important message of esteem. That we should recognize these young people are forming conclusions of morals and patriotism based on the performances of all those that served our country.

I took pictures of the schools with inclusion of school names in front of each building and tried to arrange the completion so I could super impose and image of Abraham Lincoln with stars scattered about for historic effect. In addition I had an imprint indication "Freedom Honor Flight Sept. 18, 2010" with a "Thank You" to those young people for their cards of tribute. Then I mounted it in an attractive glass frames that could be hung on the wall.

I wanted to say' "thank you' to a lot of people who treated us so well, but more so to these school children. Their ages were about seven or eight.

I envisioned mounting the cards on a support in a cluster or composition and then putting the whole thing in a frame and hanging it on the wall in my living room. At this time, I had a daydream about visiting the children at school in a supervised setting and telling them it was a wonderful experience to meet them on a personal basis to infuse them a with thoughts of doing good deeds as they grew older.

This assembly of cards would form a picture that would always remind me of the young people that wrote them in remembrance, of pride and joy, each card a personal message that implied good will and respectful acknowledgement of military service by a veteran.

The possessor of a Picasso or a Michelangelo would exalt, in gazing at Elysian artwork of untold value in my most humble perception of a great picture. I would be no less jubilant and would rejoice at my own montage. This would be my own, my Michelangelo.

Lenny
Ken

3

Kamuela

Soon after the Japanese attack at Pearl Harbor on December 7, 1941, the 40th Army Division was mobilized and embarked to Hawaii. We were encamped at Schofield Barracks; an historic Army site situated about 35 miles from Pearl Harbor.

When our ship arrived at the dock we were showered with leis, greeting from the natives with their unique music and song. This was a very nice warm welcome to their shores. This was a most pleasant occasion with a comfortable feeling of acceptance into the Hawaiian community.

At this time there was a high degree of uncertainty about the possibility of Japanese landing forces so we had to draw a conclusion that the populace was fearful of events after the attack. We were there as occupation forces and did patrols at key points around the island of Oahu.

During this time we became familiar with places on the island such as Honolulu, Diamond Head, Waikiki Beach, the Pali, (a mountain scenic pass) Kailua, a town on the opposite shore, Pearl City at the harbor and infamous Hotel Street, which I stayed away from.

It would be hard to say that one place was better than another. We found all of it pleasurable with singular songs and melodies associated with each area, rhythmic sounds that remained as enchanting memories.

So too are the names of the quaint places scattered about the island. The name seem to fit as part of a song and we heard them often, Nakul, Walpahue, Mokuleia, Kahului, Mokaku, Kawailoa and Lualualei to name a few. Dozens of other sites were equally attractive. Waikiki Beach was a must visit for everyone and to see adjacent Diamond Head.

I went to the beach and drove through those famous rolling waves. In the process I saw something unusual. Something never seen in tour guide print-outs or mentioned anywhere; beneath the surface at varying distances from shore, were ancient stone walls running parallel to the shore and spaced at distances of a hundred feet or more apart. This signified that land below the water line and beyond the shoreline was probably habitable and occupied at some earlier time and that the land subsided, or they could have been breakwater barriers. This to me was reminiscent of ancient villages found buried under the sea near the shore line in the Mediterranean.

Later we were transferred to Hawaii, the big island. If you can visualize the geography here of the piece of land eighty miles wide and about one hundred and twenty miles north to south, containing two volcano peaks just under fourteen thousand feet, namely Mauna Kea and Mauna Loa. To add to the drama they are not entirely dormant.

Although commercialism and time has made changes, the island was replete with small winding roads and a low population density which added to the feeling of being in a land strange and different. There were endless fields of pineapple and sugar cane. In Hilo some water drinking fountains emitted pineapple juice. There too were large herds of cows commonly known as the Billingham Ranch.

To get a better idea of the climate, Hawaii is about twenty degrees above the equator. Southern Arizona is thirty-two degrees north of the equator. Southern Texas at twenty-five degrees would have comparable temperatures. There is a difference though. Prevailing breezes would have a cooling effect around the islands. It took awhile to adjust to a relatively small land mass that contained two volcano peaks that rose from shore line to near fourteen thousand feet.

An area at the southern part of the island was known as Kona and was popular with tourist. It had an atmosphere all its own and grew in popularity. Because of its location it may have been protected from occasional strong winds. We occupied the island for almost a year as occupation forces. It was a waiting game. It took a long time for our forces to organize a plan together to move forward in the Pacific. Until that time, the 40 division was held at the islands.

Most of the time we were encamped at an upper elevation at the northwest part of the island, a strategic site where if needed we could be deployed quickly to any area in the north part of the island. It was sunny on most days with pleasant temperatures and fluctuating breezes. The breezes were always there. We had to get use to the idea that the wind blows in Hawaii. Up at the higher elevations the breezes conveyed a feeling of serenity.

We did not see very many natives here although there was a village of Kamuela by name, which was only that, with a few primitive huts of thatch and palm leaves. Traveling a narrow blacktop road we would at times hear the faint plink of a ukulele which seemed to tell of a timeless place or where limits on time would be alien here. Once in a while we saw two or three children playing in the sun with a woman sitting by wearing a woven hat, presiding over the activities. We waved, they waved and we moved on.

White clouds rolled around us, clinging to the side of the rising slopes. The clouds looked like large balls of cotton that we could reach out and touch. From our vantage point, we could look a long way down and see breaking surf with gigantic waves striking rock abutments sending up great sprays of water.

Some beaches were of black sand, probably from decomposed basalt which may look like obsidian, a black molten glass with no grain. Black beaches are primarily basaltic rock.

We found an old dock at Kawaihae Bay where we often went swimming in the warm water and shared it with strange fish and occasional small sting ray which were most often seen scooting along the ocean floor.

The big island is typical of the other islands as a place of wonderment and sheer beauty. The emerald green valleys and breathtaking shorelines are enchanting. I would like to experience again those balmy days and comforting breezes on my semi-clothes body. I would like to see those black sand beaches and high waves that broke in fury on the rocks. I would like to hear again that remote plink of a banjo, or ukulele which was the original Hawaiian instrument.

In 1942 this was Hawaii. This was Kamuela and desolate Kawaihae Bay before thousands of tourists invaded the scene. Before Hawaii and Kamuela were discovered, a never-never land, an unsophisticated and incredulous place. I have been fortunate to have known it then.

Until another time, 'Aloha'.

MEXICALI JAIL

4

Mexicali Iron

exicali gold could have been presumed adventure to this story, but it wasn't that way.

While living in Glendale, just north east of Los Angeles, I attended a musical one evening. It was a perfect setting with mid-summer temperatures that cooled in late afternoon. The locale was similar to an open air amphitheatre such as we think of them to be from ancient Rome.

Built in the typical semi-circular fashion on the side of a hill with successive elevated rows of seating and a central platform or state area with a back drop decorated for different scenes. In view of the mild weather, shows could be presented here thru most of the year. So as the Romans flocked to see plays and comedies we did likewise.

This particular evening the main attraction was an orchestra led by Herb Albert - born 1935. It was a well known orchestra with a unique sound. Herb Albert espoused a new sound in music with his band called, Tijuana Brass. Later I met up with another metal, mostly iron. I'll tell you about it.

The year had been tranquil for the most part. I usually drove on Sundays to Hermosa and loafed on the sandy beach. The Biltmore Hotel fronted near the shoreline and played a continuous heady musical parade of Jazz and Rock & Roll from two large loud speakers mounted on the building.

In those days we heard, Frankie Lane, Ricky Nelson, Linda Ronstadt, Chubby Checkers, Fats Domino, Frankie Avalon, Rosemary Clooney and the list goes on.

At home one day, I received a message from Ed, a friend of mine from our hometown of Chicago. He was between jobs and planned to drive to California for the summer. We made plans for a meeting on the way west. He stopped overnight in a motel in New Mexico.

It was a chilly night, not uncommon in the desert areas of the west. He was disgruntled in the morning and uncomfortable after a bad night's sleep, a result of lack of or no heat in his motel room. He left with a vengeful feeling and stole a blanket from the room. The manager called the police and a tough New Mexico Sheriff caught up with Ed on the road. He retrieved the blanket and Ed spent the night behind iron bars. Not long after, he would be looking at more iron.

We decided one weekend to run down to Mexicali in the desert on the Mexico border. It was a popular place for tourists who could have a party, drink all they want and there were no rules or curfew.

At a nearby cantina, we had some Serveza. Mexican melodies with an accordion had their own captivating lilt, easy to listen to music. I notice a narrow trough with running water at the foot rail and I did not see any evidence of a rest room. I told Ed, "We can belly up to the bar, but keep your toes out of the trough." I noticed a faint vapid odor wafting up from the floor.

We imbibed for a while absorbing the Mexican atmosphere: wooden floors that creaked, Mexican vaqueros with ten gallon hats, Mexican voices of mirth and gaiety, characterizing those who enjoyed each other's company.

Ed suddenly darted to one side and caught a local who was walking off with his hat, which had been on a wall peg. There was a tussle. Ed got his hat, the bandito yelled profane and stole into a corner. Minutes later four Mexican policio entered and threatened Ed with some vague violation. Ed walked off with him into a corner and there was a short conversation. My friend reached into a pocket, a few more words and the policio drifted away.

Ed told me the officer threatened to arrest us and we might spend a few days in jail. I was familiar with what may have been a ploy, a simple arrangement to divest the gringo of his cash.This was not unusual over the border. Mexican police don't write traffic tickets. With a mild accusation of a traffic violation, they walk away with mucho dinero.

Ed and I decided to go home. It was an eventful day, but as it played out, not a good one. The threat of jail was alarming. A peaceful period suddenly turned tremulous. We came to see the town and the bullfights but had no interest in Mexicali Iron. Especially my friend Ed, who recalls being one day late on arrival at my place after being hosted by the Albuquerque police!

5

Where Poppies Grow

One evening I saw a presentation on TV of a situation involving our military forces in the current conflict in Iraq and Afghanistan. I am not sure what segment of the service was implicated, but as I recall the Airfare was highlighted in the presentation as being privy to the manner of disposal of those killed in action.

Lacking a lot of detail I can only go on with what I saw in a brief newscast. It was about those men with bodies shattered by bombs, explosions and possible plane crashes. The devastation being so bad in some situations, only body parts were recovered and that identification with a name attributable to a person was not possible.

The sorrow at home would be immeasurable to receive an official notice of the deceased or MIA. Worse, that there was no body for burial for paying homage and last respects. This story is about body part but in its finality the body parts comprised a whole human person, a complete entity who could smile and show response and had a sense of awareness.

With the process of returning those deceased for internment something seemed to go amiss. It appeared that way, based on what I saw, although some faction may not think so. I'll tell you about it.

What I saw on TV if true, which it does appear so, was saddening to say the least. The event as portrayed jogged my memory to a time years ago when I was in a literature class in school. We had a great teacher who was so inspiring, and he discussed at one time a poem by John McRae (1872-1918). The poem was about men killed in action in World War I, in the year of about 1918, in Northern France and Germany.

Our teacher elicited a dedicated thought about how the poem showed humble reverence to the fallen men. The contents of the poem seem to have similarities with the present situation. I always remembered it because the first two lines had great impact and contained a rhythmic quality that had intonation.

Those two first lines were:

> "in Flander's fields where poppies grow
> between the crosses, row on row"

Those men passed on in 1918 in a manner as did our soldiers overseas. The columnist who wrote the story collaborated with the TV presentation. It posed a question to the Air Force, who appeared to be involved in the manner of receiving the deceased killed in action, then advising family and loved ones. At some point the proper military department would help with internment and address military honors. This protocol was as it should be for those defending our country. A body existed and was identified. I believe airfare involvement, was at least partly, due to the fact that they brought those no longer living, by air in a plane.

The question posed to the Air Force, as I saw it, was part of the program as written by the columnist. There was dialogue that the Air Force was slow and defensive in response, as though they deliberated in forming an answer.

The question to the Air Force was: how and why were they involved in a decision with the disposal of remnants of dead soldiers by dumping the body parts in a public landfill? Everywhere the hype abounds showing our respect and admiration for the American Soldier in defending our country. Organizations everywhere are doing all they can to help the returning GI to re-establish at home and get medical help as needed.

At this time I had that dramatic discourse with myself. A soliloquy that wouldn't go away. A clear feeling hard to accept and hard to believe. The idea that somewhere in our military complex a decision was made to dispose of dead soldier body pats into a landfill dump.

It would appear that the Air Force arranged with a private contractor to fulfill this finality of disposal. Apparently the Air Force could sign off to the problem with a kind of outsider support. If this is true as it appeared to be, I was appalled, and this kind of thing should never happen.

It would in my opinion be a betrayal of all that is said in defense of the military. Again lacking details this possibly may not be the whole story as it was a glimpse of a news story.

Getting back to the poem - it alludes to those values of heroic men who we must revere and represent ideals we would pursue. I would repeat John McRae's first two lines of his poem -

"in Flander's fields where poppies grow
between the crosses, row on row"

Then I became inspired and wrote my own lines. It was a feeling of joining this parade of adulation and emotional tribute.

Mute sentinels that testify
Of courageous men who came to die
A fight to be won, someone said
But history only lists the dead
A faded cause, that fails to heal
Where flags still wave, in a Flander's field

Ken Heckerson Feb 2012

6

The Cowboy Princess

Frances Octavia Smith (Dale Evans), during her early career, got a job in Louisville, Kentucky as a featured singer. She sang popular tunes like 'Shine on harvest Moon' and 'You are my Sunshine'. She lived there with her son in a third floor walk up apartment.

There followed a long list of singing radio engagements. She remarried and moved to Chicago and sang Jazz numbers at the Edgewater Beach Hotel. Later she made a better connection as featured singer with Anson Weeks Orchestra. There she sang at the Chez Pare in Chicago, IL with Ray Bolger who danced through the program, then singing New Orleans Jazz with Fats Waller.

In 1942, Frances was getting a lot of attention as an ambitious entertainer. She sang on Chase and Sanborn Hour in Chicago, starring Edgar Bergen and Charlie Mc Garthy. Frances had become known as a local songster of exceptional popularity. She was billed as a Jazz singer, the well known Blues singer, The popular songster, and Lyric Lady. She wooed the audience with

'Then Cents a Dance' Dark Town Strutters Ball, 'Ain't Misbehaving', and ' Stomping at the Savoy.'

In time, Frances was recognized as a singer of considerable talent with a remarkable range and quality of voice. She did love ballads as well as anything else, singing them smoothly and with feeling, silky and romantic quality..

So one day in 1943, I entered the Oriental Theatre to see a musical. My friend and I went back stage between acts and I was introduced to Frances. My friend was called away for half an hour.

Frances said, "I'm so thirsty, I need something to drink."

She signed her card saying 'Dear Doorman, let Ken back in. He's a friend of mine.' I put the card in my pocket. I went out the back door of the theatre to get something to drink.

I was twenty-three at the time, with lots of hair, wearing a new suit and looking good. Typical stage door Johnnies at the rear door looked me over but couldn't identify me as a celebrity. I got back with a thirst quencher and I showed the doorman the card.

For half an hour, I sat with Frances for a most enjoyable one on one private little chit-chat that I will never forget. She was thirty-one at the time.

I was not fully aware of her rising popularity although I knew it was her show and she was the featured singer. My friend returned shortly. I voiced admiration to Frances and she went back on stage.

After her marriage to Roy Rogers, the cowboy star in 1947, she played heroine in many western movies and was titled, "the Cowboy Princess." Before her marriage she was professionally known as, Dale Evans.

Dale had a Down Syndrome child which inspired her in 1953 to write a book "Angel Unaware." It was on the New York best seller list for four months with thirty printings. All proceeds were donated to the "National Association for Retarded Children." Fifty years after publication, the book still earned seven to twelve thousand dollars.

Roy Rogers 1911-1998
Dale Evans 1912-2001

Footnote: "Happy Trails" movie with Roy Rogers was on location at Vasquez Rocks as I wrote of in my story called "The Renegade Dude."

7

The Bunsen burner BBQ

I was about sixteen years of age at the time of this story, which occurred in 1935. An incident or better called an accident which remains as an unwanted memory.

Without question, this particular experience was frightening and overwhelming and can easily qualify as "my most embarrassing moment'.

Ray, a friend of mine was attending an evening trade school class and I accompanied him one night as a guest and observer. Earlier we had secured permission from Miss Evelyn, the teacher. The evening sessions focused on laboratory equipment and techniques, at the high school level. Based on the presumption of having interest in this subject, I envisioned entry into the class in the following semester.

Miss Evelyn as we referred to her seemed to fit the stereotype of that well known image of a young, about twenty-two years of age, ebullient, and attractive "school marm'. She had a clear strong voice with good articulation and that special ability to explain and clarify which seemed to be a necessary adjunct to good teaching.

Although the class was held in a large room, the cluster of students, mostly boys, was confined to a central area of seating. The chairs 8 desks were mounted to the floor and consisted of about six rows with adequate space for walking between the rows.

I don't recall if this was the first day of class but some time elapsed in naming each student and to get an idea why he or she had an interest in the subject. I was introduced as a onetime guest and received a warm welcome. The term 'warm' could truly be held as mild in view of what was about to happen.

In time past I recalled a similar demonstration in a classroom which involved a display of glass bowls, tubes and siphons and strange odors from odious containers. One in particular to the best of my memory includes exposure of sulfur and some other noxious element that resulted in a never to be forgotten odor very remindful of rotten eggs. That demo stayed with me for a long time.

As Miss Evelyn moved a few glass containers around and fiddled with a Bunsen burner, a faded memory of a nauseating rotten egg odor became reminiscent. She embarked on an explanation or discourse of the nature of burning gasses and how in some instances oxygen is part of the formula introduced with a gas to either cause a flame or burning effect. She made brief references to several materials that although flammable varied in volatility.

The Bunsen burner was designed to burn with a non-luminous flame by mixing air with the gas or volatile fluid at the base of the burner. It was invented by Robert Wilhelm Bunsen (1811-1899) and was used for heating substances in the laboratory.

It consisted of a metal tube on a stand and a long rubber hose that connects the tube to the gas jet. Adjusted openings at the base of the tube controlled the amount of air that mixed with the gas. The Burning process was smokeless except that it can and does produce a wavering blue tip of flame well beyond the jet, so that there is an intervening column of gas and oxygen (hardly visible) that feeds the blue flame. The blue tip is clear evidence of fire and that something is burning.

No doubt the inventor envisioned countless lab exercises with this Bunsen burner that would be integral as an aid to science in multitudinous ways. I believe if he were aware of the potential for ill advised activities and in particular the mishap on my part with a Bunsen burner his countenance would evoke arched eyebrows and quizzical apprehension.

So it was with me, a miss adventure that reduced my own personal esteem to one of abashment and humiliation.

Miss Evelyn approached the front row of students slowly with a handheld manila folder, atop which sat a lit Bunsen burner. As she walked up and down each row, the students were enable a close look at the nature of the flame. As she approached my chair, I was intrigued by the surreptitious blue flame that moved about forming different shapes, often seeming to disappear and then re-appearing, but always detached from the jet several inches away.

This innocuous space appeared as an odd adjunct to a live flame as the intervening space showed no evidence of burning. I was curious. I did what no other had done. I put my hand up and extended a finger into this so-called column of gas. Was there heat or burning there? All was quiet. Everyone gazed at the burner, and the blue tip of flame. Then the most frightening thing that could happen did happen.

The quiet moment exploded into a nightmare of fiasco. A scene I wish I could have forgotten. In a moment I was looking at a conflagration, a shower of flame and in the midst of it, Miss Evelyn was on fire!

Reaching out to the burner, my finger tipped it over and a liquid gas poured over Miss Evelyn. Her dress went up in flames like the Hindenburg. So did her petticoat. Her stockings were reduced to shapeless bits of cloth. There was a mild roaring noise as the bulk of the gas burned. Snapping noises ensued and surrounding flames devoured her clothing. Burnt shreds hung loosely and distended from her body. For a stunning moment, the fire and smoke had engulfed her.

Recovering from this visual shock we all ran to her and beat her body with our hands to pound out and smother remaining flame and sparks. She remained upright and possibly calm. At this point I was not sure of her condition or composure.

As the sparks and burning subsided, bits of burnt fabric floated around, wavering and moving haphazardly, wafted about by small currents of air. The smell of burnt clothing was acrid and pungent. I was afraid her hair caught fire but it did not. Beating the sparks and flame took awhile.

As the danger seemed to subside, an image emerged somewhat skewed from an earlier time. Miss Evelyn must have been aware of what we saw. It was complete disarrangement. Our teacher's dress and petticoat was completely gone. There were a few taters of what were undergarments and patches of skin showed in places.

Miss Evelyn walked to a nearby closet plucking at remnants of burnt fiber. In view of everyone and with no attempt to hide anything, she pulled a dress off a hanger and squirmed into it. At this time, she had good composure.

I walked over to her and started to apologize. I was abashed and had no idea how she would respond.

She said, "It's alright. It was just an accident."

I thought she had poise and emotional control.

Then I left the building with Ray. I was still impacted by what happened. I looked and walked in a rather straight ahead fashion and dimly knew it would be some time before I would be feeling normal. Our partially unclothed teacher and fire and smoke were a mild shock.

I asked Ray, "Do you think she is alright?"

He was a little older than I.

He responded, "Sure, she looks alright."

I told him, "I'm not."

8

The Murphy Bed

Some time ago I was exposed to an incident that may have been a challenge. There are times when an incident calls for valor or strength of conviction, but situations vary, as does the measure of a person.

Many times I have questioned my own ability to act in a positive manner. Men in military service have shown great courage for which they were honored and bestowed with medals of recognition. Life is full of challenges. Whether is be a jobber decision with health, commitments are made. In the game of poker it's a constant challenge to determine if your cards are good enough to stay in the game or if you have to call and bow out of that hand. Of course some situation are trivia and in my case I may have been lucky not to have seen too many life threatening situations. Yes, there were difficult times when parents died and kinfolk passed on, or a loved one was gone. I might have been a weasel in some situations but hopefully not always. One incident remains in my memory bank as (fond remembrance). I'll tell you about it.

My story started while I was living in Los Angeles. I had been going to Lawrence Weeks Polka dances at the Aragon Ballroom on Lick Pier in Oceanside. I met a girl there and we had a few dances and a soda together. I liked her, she seemed to be my type, not flagrant, but pleasant, a bit reserved with seemingly good manners. All those Saturday nights at the Aragon ran late so after leaving we hunted down my favorite all night cafe for little thin buttermilk pancakes. Invariably movie stars were seen there so we had an extra treat, like seeing another show. Sometimes it might have been a secondary luminary but on occasion a top flight performance.

My dance partners name was Roberta. After we left the cafe I followed her car to her place and walked right in with her. It was a bit compact like an efficiency and that is typically where you find the Murphy bed which is an affair that is spring loaded and with a light touch folds up out of the way into the wall. We sat and talked on a small divan. She told me she came from a small town in Michigan. I told her I grew up in Chicago, but was born in England and had been living in California for five years with my mother who died recently. My mother (Annie) was buried at Forest Lawn in Glendale among many deceased movie stars.

Could it have been the start of a romance? We exchanged addresses and phone numbers and subsequently she visited my place several times.

As we were both single we each had small apartments. My landlady lived below my apartment and I wondered if she had thoughts about the visits. I didn't care much because I had already absorbed some of the California life-style which is from a sociological standpoint functional as compared to the midwest which is traditional. One interpretation of functional is just doing what works. This must be a far cry from the Victorian age but that California. This might be a residual condition of the early pioneers who were brave and fearless and made their own standards for living.

I had a small RV and we took a jaunt following the ridge north of San Berdoo. This was just west of the Mojave Desert following a gradual rise in elevation. The exact route escapes me but it had to be almost five hundred miles to Stateline at Lake Tahoe which borders on Carson City in Nevada, just south of Reno. At Stateline we turned west and went down the west slope of the Sierra Mountains through historic Placerville into the San Joaquin Valley into Sacramento. We ate real sheepherder bread, procured in small villages and enjoyed vast panoramas and vistas of great beauty.

In Sacramento we wandered into a park and sat under a big shade tree. We both knew what we felt. It was a day of reckoning and parting of the ways. It was an ominous moment. We had enjoyed each others companionship for several weeks and were just getting used to each other. I liked Roberta. She could be my kind of girl. I though we were compatible.

I told Roberta I would go back to Milwaukee and look for a job. I had lost my current job recently. I had no trade other than sales experience and seriously had doubts about employment in California. She did not want to go back to her old neighborhood in Michigan and preferred to stay in California. I thought she was brave and positive with the typical California pioneer attitude. Especially being single and on her own. I know then it was a challenge and a difficult one. Going back to Milwaukee, in retrospect, was a mistake. I lost California and Roberta too, for which I have always had great regret.

The sad part of the blossoming friendship was the fact that we probably could have managed temporary problems. We could have gotten married and lived happily ever after, but it was not to be. I have always viewed it as the wrong call. We should have stayed together and very important was her attitude of compliance. I believe not having a job was the important factor in looking the other way.

I often think of that momentous time with Polka music and Robertas pleasant voice, and when I followed her into her place where she lived and we talked of trivia. Being a small apartment I probably didn't notice she had a Murphy bed. She told me then about her family and the small town in Michigan. I told her I grew up in Chicago but was born in England, and when I came to

California I brought my mother with me because she had no place to live. Our conversation dwindled and there was a long moment of silence. Then Roberta broke the silence, "Well Ken, are you going to pull the bed down?" That was not the Pepsi Challenge. It was my call.

P.S. This is a story of something good staring in your faced you don't know it.

Holding hands for what I know
Was in her eyes, a loving glow
What torch did wield the greatest bond
Through misty air — a magic wand
This love light in the afterglow
For us a path, where it has led
Agreed and true, we have tried
She said, love me now, or love me never
Then life slipped by, love lost forever

Ken Heckerson Sept 2013

9

The Inside Story

This might be called a sequel to my story (God Almighty) where we find characters with something in common, from a similar habitat. Everyone would like to hear the inside story. Everyone would like to hear the inside story. The truth about what appears normal on the surface but what is behind the scene doesn't not always show. To say it another way, 'what you see is not always what you get'.

This would apply to magicians of course, that's their stock in trade. It's fun to be fooled when we expect it. Unfortunately there are other magicians around like card sharks, conmen and the so-called fast pitch salesman, supposedly from the past, but I'm not sure about that.

Auto salesmen have a poor image but it just might be the nature of the business that puts the salesman in a bad position. The problem is to give the customer a fair deal and at the same time defend a price that could render some margin of profit, so it is easy to see the customer can be part of the problem.

I can be deviating here from the main character in this story. The who can serve up an item of great quality but at times, something less. My reference is my experience with professional chefs, barkeeps and food servers. At this point, I must retreat a bit to say, no, most people have the best intentions and not the so-called magician. They just get caught in difficult situations and bend the rules for expediency.

It's hard to believe a recent story I saw in The Tribune. I thought refilling a brand name whiskey bottle with cheaper stuff was an old trick, but they are still doing it. It was a well known food chain in New Jersey (probably a franchise) that served liquor. They perpetrated this old hoax and got caught. A really cheap stunt.

Some years ago, my wife worked at a country club. Her specialty was salads and desserts. Country club members were a kind of select clientele so the food had to be good. At one special occasion catering to a large group she had to make an appetizer which called for gelatin in the recipe. It was wormy, and she went to the kitchen manager for a change. As usual this was a stressful moment. He growled 'use it'. She objected. He looked at his watch and repeated with force, 'do it now or it's your job'. She did it now.

At another time in a different country club she was forced to quit her job. The chef tried to have sex with her every morning.

In another scene she told me a customer sent a steak back a second time. Still too rare. The chef was enraged. He threw it on the floor and jumped on it, then put it back in a frying pan.

Not too long ago, I read where a barkeep filled an order for two mixed drinks. He had his own version but was caught urinating in both glasses.

About two years ago, I read where two New York policemen ordered hamburgers in a fast food place and caught a food server spitting in both sandwiches.

I've worked in several kitchens and it seems to be the order of the day to ignore hair nets. Managers think the rules are too bothersome to enforce. What we see more often are baseball caps and lots of flowing hair, or not nets or caps at all.

At opportune times to see in the kitchen, I still note an absence of gloves when they should be worn. Touching and moving food on a plate with bare hands is a no-no, but it happens often. What irritates me is a food server arriving with a plate of food with a thumb in it.

It seems lately kitchen workers are washing hands like they are supposed to. Once I saw an employee leave the restroom and he did not wash his hands. How did I know? I was in the rest room at the time.

There are reasons why managers look the other way. They have to be sure before making a reprimand, and reluctant to fire someone of the expense and time to train a new employee. Managers also want and need cooperation from coworkers who are not to be viewed as recalcitrant or difficult.

While living in Milwaukee, I read a story about a little girl who died of a condition of cross contamination. A kitchen worker used a knife to cut raw meat and on the same cutting board used the same knife for cutting raw food for salads. This is a basic rule never ever violated but it happened. A contamination from the raw meat and caught up in salad. It was a high profile place to eat. It was closed and shut down in a few weeks. How could this accident waiting to happen get by the chef? Using the same cutting board would be a red flag even before incident. Was a Chef not diligent? Were the workers property indoctrinated to basic kitchen rules for food safety? The court must have heard it all.

Once at Perkins Restaurant, I saw a waitress cough and sneezed twice. She was standing near a table of six people ready to eat. If a worker is ill they should be sent home but more often than not the problem is ignored. Germs are everywhere and are in the air. A sneeze could expel germs six or eight feet.

If I was at this table, I would be apprehensive. The rule book is usually adhered to in normal conditions. When time is short, or a lack of help, a normal situation can become stressful. That is when difficult decisions are made and the aftermath might be in doubt. Some places are very careful, because a bad decision could be disastrous.

I worked in a supper club in Milwaukee. Their motto was if in doubt, throw it out. They did their best every day to appease a hungry customer.

I would like to repeat, most people do their best and it could be to defend their own reputation as a good worker in addition to having respect for a customer, who in a sense, is paying the bill. Unfortunately, things happened in the kitchen which is not part of the plan. In the digital world, they might call it a glitch.

Unknown Chefs - we overlook
Just give the order to the cook
There simply is no guarantee
What we get is what we see
Goodness served for you and others
Could it be as good as mothers
What queen said 'give them cake'
When peasants stormed the royal gate
A fast food mess from the kitchen
Just enjoy & quit the bitch'n
If it doesn't suit your taste
Fay, send it not, back in haste
Whatever good God hath wrought
A primo cook could render naught
Stay, chef's sanctum, it is said
Where even angels fear to tread

Ken Heckerson Sept 2013

10

The Peasant

In our history we've had a variety of people symbolic in some way: aliens, ex-patriots, ex-husbands, migrants, pioneers and list goes on. They all stand apart in some way and for a reason or cause. Things happened, conditions changed to the extent that for someone a different kind of life evolved, in some situations a destiny not altogether planned.

In a sociology class one day we were discussing hunger and how the masses cope with it. Out of this conversation a symbolic person evolved. Our instructor dwelled on the activities in a primitive society and said that in that environment most people spent most of their active day searching for food. This then was what we came to know as the classic definition of that person in a particular group or class of people (the peasant).

I thought about it for a while and it seemed to me that possibly modern society has a connection. Most of us work all week to earn a paycheck which is then used to buy a variety of things, presumably most of it for sustenance which includes food. Are we peasants by another name?

What seems to prevail is a condescending or patronizing attitude toward the designation of a peasant that it denotes a lower class in the society or something less than who we personally think we are.

It has always been common knowledge that in society some people derive satisfaction in knowing that they are better in some way than someone else. This may be real or perceived but either way it supports a viewers feeling of inadequacy and supports an ego that could be weak in terms of a standard that it should be. Viewing the peasant might be supportive to feeling important and extend a feeling of confidence in themselves.

Regardless of our attitudes about wealth we live in a materialistic environment and to ignore it is tantamount to saying we don't get it. Yet we must agree to strive for values that are attainable as virtues, being charitable and humane, are within our grasp. Ideals we strive for as well as wealth. It remains, we find satisfaction in paying bills are settling an imbalance in our lives. This has a tendency to satisfy our relationship in society and in the spiritual sphere.

In our every day life a godly presence is our guide but we still have to deal with others here on earth. It seems those others have made some of the rules we live by. Hopefully we make the best effort for success with coexistence with our fellow man. It remains that we should be a protective entity. We are enriched as receivers of friendly gestures, praise, goodwill and benevolence. Something likewise should emanate from each one of us, call it a positive force. It could be charity, an art form that people enjoy, or a message that conveys joy or happiness. I think the so-called peasant could qualify in one form or another for all of the above. As peasants it would appear to me we are capable of good things.

This original image of the peasant was based largely on the early European scene which was agricultural and food was found in trees and crops and varied growth out of the ground in the marketplace. In Europe a common expression to denote something less, was the expression of the Tourista. In a sense true, as it inferred a person out of his natural habitat and probably not so sure of his surroundings. The expression was to some extent demeaning. In France too, a popular reference toward a minority group or class was the expression of bourgeois, pronounced buzhwazi. This was the commoner or working blue collar class. It was meant to be derogatory and with some contempt.

So today it appears that the reference to a peasant is rather demeaning but shouldn't be. It could be mentioned today with a sense of humor although still a bit degrading.

In some of John Wayne's western movies he made reference to pilgrims in his conversations, probably with the same meaning. I still wonder, in essence are we all peasants behind a facade that blurs that image.

It's obvious we can't call a rich man a peasant because he must have been productive in some manner, even if he did not contribute to society. So I perceive in our society that a peasant is more likely to be poor or of little wealth. Again it seems that the material concept affects our judgment. It seems to be relegated to where our values are and that there are still virtues in being a peasant. A peasant could be simply lazy and not disposed to any effort. At the same time an industrious peasant may not be desirous of wealth as we know it.

In India the most admired people, at least in history, were those who owned nothing more than a robe, a bowl and a cane. A vast difference to values of our own. Can there be a reconciliation to value so far apart. There is a strong correlation here with the well-known agricultural peasant in Europe.

In the USA a peasant gets no kudos, if he is not productive for a wealth or some material value. I could probably go to India and receive some esteem as a peasant. I would still have to put some funds together to pay for passage, but with little effort I might blend with the crowd and still retain some respect.

Exodus is not rare. It happens for a reason or other. Going to India is feasible. A strong enough conviction is the motivator. India is crowded but they say there is always room for one more. I would bid, see you there.

There's a place, its near Tibet
You could get there in a jet
Travel light with robe and bowl
Bring a stick to poke a hole
If in U.S. you are mired
Go where you can be admired
A region known for sacred cows
You can join with solemn vows
Can it be a better place
To live a life, not in haste
To find, it might be unpleasant
A native knows, ask a peasant

Ken Heckerson March 2012

11

Bigfoot

Over many decades a variety of stories have emerged about Bigfoot with reactions of apprehension, disbelief, fearfulness and even acceptance that he or it is real. Most stories seem to relate to a remote area like the Himalaya Mountains in Asia or here in the western part of the country in isolated places in Montana.

What would be seemingly strange and worthy of concern were recent reports of seeing Bigfoot in a populated area, no less than Griffith Park in Southern California and only a few miles from Hollywood and Beverly Hills. These reports emanated as a kind of rumor or comments from neighbors about something that slithered about in the bushes and always faded out of sight in the foilage. The stories caused doubt and concern with planned visits to the park.

In recent times there were memos and odd items in local newspapers which engendered feelings of curiosity and wonderment. A phenomena not well received in and around Griffith Park. It is a vast expanse with numerous small trails, roads running in different directions with a maze of hills, valleys, gulches and deep ravines, an area that presents itself as one that is better looked upon rather than to walk through.

The usual visitors are picnickers, hikers, boy scout groups and the occasional tourist. It is a place of scenic wonder with large groups of trees and heavy vegetation, a departure from the general condition of sand and sparse foliage due to the geographic location that is largely semi-arid in climate. Due to the size of the park people at times have come lost and were discovered that night or following day, wandering in a fruitless search for an exit or point of origin.

The time was long past when Indians and the furious outlaws rode horseback through the area. Nearby Vasquez Rocks was a famous hideout for a Mexican bandit but fear and apprehension now was another concern. No less the apprehension of Bigfoot. There were those who claimed he had been seen.

Rising curiosity and rumor called for response from the local chief of police who stated that there was no Bigfoot in Griffith Park and laid it to rumor, idol talk and unsubstantiated comments.

During a visit that I made to the park I saw signs with the directive I had never seen in any park. They read "No minors allowed in the park without an adult." This to me conveyed an implication. Of what, I could not ascertain. Was Bigfoot in the park? Was the report by the police simply one to allay the public. Maybe people would start bringing weapons to the park and permissive shooting could have serious aftermath. If the police did suspect something like Bigfoot it would be plausible that they were looking for him. If so, they were doing it in a covert way.

Overtime I concluded that there could be predators in the park. For one reason or other an unsuspecting person could be easy prey for one intent to rob or assault.

A recent report received by the police entailed a family group out for a picnic. It was a holiday. Two tables were set up and they were preparing to eat. The aroma of barbecue filled the air. Suddenly two shots rang out. They sounded like pistol shots from near by bushes. One bullet struck a wooden table support. The other made a sharp shattering noise as it passed through a metal garage container. The people fled in fright, leaving everything behind.

Did Bigfoot carry a gun? Was Bigfoot a human or animal? If animal, then there would be no gun.

Due to the mild climate in this part of the country transients and homeless persons are numerous, and drift in a kind of aimless pattern. A social phenomena that indigenous people are well aware of. When shots are fired it is no longer a subject of simple conversation.

The police department knew something the public was not aware of. Overtime they had reports of picnickers being shot at and alarmed to the extent, they fled for their lives. A few attempts to find perpetrators yielded nothing.

Now there was a resurgence of these reports. Two detectives were dispatched to observe and explore the area. During midsummer at a picnic a shot was fired. The detectives saw a furtive figure. It was near evening and the sky was darkening but the chase was on. Heavy thickets, difficult terrain, a trail not clear. The pursuit ended at the bottom of a ravine at the foot of a cliff.

A manlike figure disappeared into a recess in the face of the cliff. The detectives advanced cautiously. After a few moments they emerged with a disheveled bodily form of a large man although somewhat emaciated, with heavy beard, and a tangled mass of longhair covering his face. His ragged unkempt appearance was a forlorn figure, a product of survival in a primitive environment. Patches of skin showed through holes in the tattered mis-matched clothing. Offering no resistance an abject and frightened man, a question of identity surfaced in facial expression.

At the station they tried to calm the man they had captured. He was alone and depicted a loner, for whatever reason living outside the realm of society. somewhere, sometime in the past he drifted from the community and fashionable world, and lived in a cave in a remote area of the park.

Although his speech was not clear it was determined that he fired the pistol at people to frighten them away. He would then take the food. There was no intent to harm anyone. He was fed and given new clothing and subsequently confined to mental rehab, and his future was unknown.

Picnickers now dallied and reveled in peaceful enjoyment. The menace of oft spoke Bigfoot was now known to be no other than the cave dweller at Griffith Park. The presence of Bigfoot subsided and he was heard of no more.

12

The Cardboard Box Campout

It was not easy to start this story. It was an epic event with lots of confusion and excitement. Such was the case when on October 1, 1932 the New York Yankees came to Chicago to play the Cubs for game 3 at Wrigley Field.

When the word Americana is used it means many things to many people. Close to the hearts of all classes across the nation it means things like apple pie, picnics, birthday parties, valedictories, homemade lemonade, and the list goes on. We could add baseball to the list.

When the Yankees arrived with a team member, the much vaunted Babe Ruth, the air was electric. That was the day he vanquished the Cubs. It was also a day to forever place baseball in the same special hall of tradition know as Americana.

It was not unusual for the crowds to be out of control. Chicago is a sports minded place and it is always very evident. There were never enough entrances to absorb the rush of fans. Congestion was everywhere, with a high noise level due to all the yelling, police whistles, auto traffic, scalpers, and hawkers and a milling throng, all running in different directions. Such is game day.

To say that some fans arrived early would be an understatement. One avid customer set on a cracker box since the day before (he was front in line) so he was the first to enter the bleachers. A virtual encampment was a conglomerate line of big cardboard boxes, curtains, bed sheets, canvas covers, canopies, cushions, folding beds, and oversized umbrellas, all strung out along the park wall for several hundred yards. A thousand people or more camped out for three days in advance of the game.

Bereft of finer housing a few slept on the sidewalk in sleeping bags or blankets. Two girls had a makeshift bed. They alternated guarding the bed while the other ran for hotdogs, peanuts and soda. Local Taverns and cafés were engulfed with visitors, to use the restrooms. Vehicle traffic was so bad the traffic signals were shut off, and policeman directing traffic. Those in the far away upper levels were called "bleacher bums" and the moniker never went away.

Dedication to the game was high ethics. A former cardinal first baseman Keith Hernandez said, "What a beautiful ball yard. I wouldn't be surprised if they're standing at attention in their apartments to during the anthem and the stretch. The neighborhood is part of the game and the game is part of the neighborhood."

There were a few not afraid of heights who watch the game from trees across the street. Most fans including kids from schools waited along the outside walls of the park playing in groups or just looking for a free ticket to the bleachers or to crash the park. In some instances aggressive and eager (no fear) youngsters have climbed the walls when the police wandered elsewhere. Some cops threw their nightsticks at them. Some were caught in daring resistance and tossed back at them. They knew the police would not climb the wall and they had it made if they got over the top, providing they did not encounter a guard on the inside.

Friday was a special day, Ladies Day. It was a day when excess emotions show a capability not normally seen. In a statement by an official to the Saturday Evening Post he said,"It is easier to control 100,000 men than of 10,000 women." William Wrigley (owner) found that no matter what he did, the ladies who crashed the gates for free on selected days were surprisingly rough.

The ladies listen to a speech urging them to take their time and assuring them that each applicant will be accommodated, then they storm wickets (a small door or window or a ticket cage), sweeping aside policeman and guards in a way to make men gasp, and wonder how the phrase "The gentler sex" ever originated.

What they do to one another in the process of crashing the gate is astounding, even to the male spectators. So the young men storm the walls and perched on top to view the game. The woman storm the gates. The cardboard box campers were first in line and had the edge, but they spent a few sleepless nights in the process.

Wrigley did not want to say that on Ladies Day that ladies couldn't still be recognized as a "high tea" and "peaches and cream set." Although he said later that he could not get a policeman to go up there. We had to drive them up because if a man talks back to a policeman or a usher he could get a punch in the nose. But a woman can say anything with impunity and they abuse these fellows something terrible. That's the Chicago crowd. Very implicit, very direct. So much for the Ladies Day.

At the big game on October 1, 1932 the fans were squatting in cardboard boxes three days before the gates opened. Bleacher tickets sold for $1.10 and went on sale as of 6:30 AM. Standing room tickets sold for $2.50. All bleacher seats were sold out by 1230. It was game 3 of the series. The Yankees won the first two. 49,986 fans were present. The Yankees jumped ahead 3 to 0 in the first inning, and the rally included a three run home run by Babe Ruth. Fans who disliked him through lemons at him.

In the fourth inning the Cubs tied the game which set the stage for one of baseballs most famous home runs. In the fifth inning the Babe hit a monstrous fly ball, a homer into the centerfield bleachers. This was his famous called shot. It sailed past the flagpole on the right side of the centerfield scoreboard and hit the box office at the corner of Waveland and Sheffield Avenues. As Ruth rounded the bases he yelled and cursed at the Cubs bench. Later seven different people claimed to have the ball he drove out of the park. This was the famous hit where he apparently or supposedly pointed to where he was going to hit the ball. A sign of extreme confidence, but the pointing sign has always been debatable. Questioned a year later he said "No" he did not point, but it might have been a negative gesture toward the Cubs dugout.

Following the Yankee win of 7 to 5 they hosted Bill "Bojangles" Robinson in their locker room. Robinson danced on top of a trunk while the New York Yankees yelled and clapped their hands.

In all of it a day of bedlam, police patrols, arrests, surreptitious scalpers, hawkers, fans with no tickets but selling a line position, winners and losers. The cardboard box campers saw a great show.

In the aftermath, perhaps Shirley Povitch, a sports writer of the Washington Post said it best, "Who could ever forget the scene, even if he never saw it."

13

The PJ Disaster

As this tale unfolds, it could be called 'The Hot Pants Fiasco'. At this point, a reader may contour a romance that could be known as a relationship or with reference to being a steamy affair. Although the title may be misleading, there is some truth and substance to it, but with a different scenario.

If I said there was a day of fire in my PJs it could support my mentioned comments. It has been said all the world loves a love story and I wish this was one. To think about the joy and happiness that accompanies ardent love, with the sharing of sublime intimacy, is a wonderful emotion to feel and to be happy for those so entwined.

With some hesitancy and misgivings about a fantasy that maybe churning in the minds of my readers, I must render some apology in saying there was no torrid affair, no romance and no exalted moments. In a simple straight forward statement, I wish to tell what really happened knowing all the while the absence of an amours liaison could be disappointing. I remember the time quite well. I still cringe at the thought, it was the day my PJs caught fire.

Tumbling out of bed and groping and fumbling around seems to be a daily routine I follow for a few minutes of every day. Years ago I would sprightly bounce out of bed with a kind of eagerness and vitality to meet the challenge of a new day. Lately things have changed a bit and my movements have been slower and more methodical.

One day I wandered into the kitchen, still not fully awake and poured a small glass of orange juice. I gazed at the ceiling for a while turning over in my mind what I would like for breakfast. After eating corn flakes for four days, I wanted something else.

I didn't know it then, but I was getting very close to a hazard that would suddenly make me very wide awake. Surprising how in a moment of time I was transformed from a not alert kind of lethargic to one of being hyper and wide awake.

Hearing and vision are probably the most anticipatory sensors that send a signal to the brain, calling for a response or action. I was about to get a vivid visional signal, not TV. I never turn it on in the morning, no irritating fruit flies that came with a bunch of grapes I bought. There was no sudden ray of sunlight shining through a cloud. It was the lull before the storm.

It was a chilly morning and the temperature in the apartment was cold. I always turn the thermostat down at bedtime. To warm things up, I opened the oven door and set the control to 200 degrees. The heating element heats to max and then shuts off until the thermostat calls for heat when the oven temperature goes below 200 degrees. It warms up the kitchen nicely.

I noticed a pan in the oven which I attempted to remove. It was hot. I pulled it out with a towel. Suddenly I smelled something burning and saw lighted embers in the air… the towel was on fire, flames rampant. When reaching for the pan a corner of the towel had touched a heat rod in the bottom of the oven.

While standing in a moment of stupefaction, holding the towel at my side, I discovered I was burning. My PJ's were on fire! The hairs on my legs were singed. I beat the towel madly and at the same time fought desperately to get out of the burning PJs!

I fought the flame, I fought time, and I fought against being overwhelmed by a debacle. The lower half of my PJ's were gone. My legs were hairless.

I sat down exhausted, looking for stray embers of glowing fire. In a different scenario, I thought there could be a better way to lose my PJs.

14

Confessions of a Carbohydrate Addict

It was a revelation for me to read recently how the popular theory of free radicals devastate our bodies and how antioxidants defend to keep us healthy. It is apparently an ongoing conflict that can sometimes overwhelm a persons health. I felt satisfied this was sufficient as a negative force I need to look no further at debilitating activity in our body. Not so.

In another area a particularly innocent kind of lifestyle can be cause for dilemma. I discovered that having a great taste for pasta and breads and a cavalcade of related starches, snack foods and sweets was detrimental to my health.

As an auto can do a 180 degree turn I have likewise mad a turn on a road less traveled to achieve a new kind of quest for health. You may know it as "confessions of a carbohydrate addict."

I have been fortunate not to have some of the typical problems such as a continuous craving for junk food and sweets, eating when you don't need to, or eating too much, and did not take any drugs for the problem. Regardless I was just consuming altogether too many, too much carbs. What affected me and changed my diet were scientist statements about the hi-carb diet. These assertions alone were sufficient to make a change.

I reacted in a similar fashion (abruptly) years ago when I got sick one morning after a breakfast of fried food. It was the beginning of what was probably a stomach ulcer according to my doctor, who attributed it primarily to my smoking habit of two packs a day. He said if I want to recover, I must give up fried food, coffee, beer or Jack Daniels, or other items that would encourage worsening of the ulcer. I quit that day and never took another cigarette.

I must add a psychological factor. I did not want to accept the idea that a small inanimate object (a cigarette) was a force stronger than my own conviction to fight it. Being a neuromuscular habit I did things to satisfy the habit. I put a cigarette in my mouth but didn't light it. Eat a cookie or chew gum. A variety of things to fool the habit. In three months the nicotine had left my body and with it the strong cravings.

Learning about hi-carbs was the same scenario. Bad news. I didn't like what appeared ahead. The decision was not easy. Growing up in Chicago I made many trips to one of our favorite shops, Carlson's Bakery, and came home with a bagful of chocolate eclairs, French cream puffs, Swedish coffee cakes, succulent doughnuts and streusel topped offerings. Now it was more difficult to refrain and look away from those tempting pastry creations. Delicacies that could arouse a passion like no other.

A sobering side to this fantasy and this inclination to indulge in hi-carb taste treats, are the stern admonitions from nutrition authorities conveying a story of caution, a message that carbs in excess with an outward goodness are culprits that will shorten your life among other mis-adventures. Exponents of health have things to say, a reality check, if you care to read and listen.

Some terms ascribed to the subject:

- Diabetes Type 1 - Insulin dependent, pancreas no longer makes insulin. There is no survival without insulin.
- Diabetes Type 2 - Body cells do not respond properly to available insulin to allow entry of glucose, known as "insulin resistant," non-insulin dependent.
- Hyperglycemia - Too much insulin, too much food.
- Hypoglycemia - Too little sugar in the blood, resulting in insulin reaction, shock.
- Soluble Fiber - Dissolves in water.
- Insoluble Fiber - Does not dissolve in water, not digestible, no calories
- Glycemic Index - A scale to measure ability of carbo foods to elevate blood sugar and insulin levels.

• Triglycerides - Thicken blood and retard flow, a storage fat, a risk factor for heart disease, elevated triglycerides come from overconsumption of refined carbohydrates and is correctable by restriction of carbohydrates.
• Glucose - A form of sugar
• Plaque - fatty deposit buildup in artery, atherosclerosis
• Tans-fat -Partially hydrogenated oil, dangerous, polyunsaturated oil processed to make solid at room temperature, cardiovascular disease, sooner than later, known as a molecular misfit, the human body not designed to handle it.
• Refined Carbs - Sugar, high fructose corn syrup, skim milk, fruit juice, dried fruit, white flour (no nutrition), baked goods, pasta and other starchy foods like baked potato and white rice.
• Simple Carbs - Sugars, milk lactose, glucose, fruits and vegetables, fructose, sucrose (also known as cane or beet sugar). Also found in candy, fruit drinks, milk, sugar coated cereals, honey, syrup, preserves and desserts.
• Complex Carbs - Bread, pasta, rice, beans, potatoes, corn, peas, carrots, beets and broccoli.
• Glycosylation - sticky glucose molecules, exposure to excess glucose.

It's interesting to see how the three food groups function. Carbohydrates are converted to glucose which is metabolized or "burned" for energy.

Proteins are converted to amino acids which provide building blocks for bone, muscle and tissue. Fats become fatty acids burned for energy or stored as body fat. Fat is burned differently form glucose producing ketones, an anacetone body involved in acidosis, a function in metabolism.

I saw a TV program that linked excess glucose, diabetes 2, with Alzheimers. Read what Dr Atkins said in 2001, "Excess blood sugar or ages (advanced glycosylation) tend to form clumps of cross linked proteins that are very similar to the tangles and plaques found in the brains of Alzheimers patients. Found at 3 times the level in normal brains suggesting that they are responsible at least in part for the progression of Alzheimers. Reducing carbs lowers blood pressure, bringing blood glucose and insulin to better levels."

Other Medical Quotes:

"Eating the typical high carb diet forces the body constantly to produce large amounts of insulin to cope with all the glucose. The insulin converts it to fat." Robert C. Atkins MD

T.L. Cleave, a British surgeon predicted after twenty years of eating high carb foods, diabetes and heart disease would begin to appear. Atkins supports the statement.

"Patients changed to low carb diet, reversed or reduced heart disease and related aspects of aging." Robert C. Atkins MD

"Blood sugar control is at the core of any age defying program." And, "Elevations in blood sugar produce more free radicals." Robert C. Atkins MD

"Diabetes is 3rd leading fatal disease, the leading cause of blindness, end stage kidney failure, lower extremity amputations, and leading risk factor for heart disease and strokes. Beyond, is emotional cost and financial cost." And an interesting statement, "Scientists believe the onset of most cases of Diabetes 1 is caused by deficient immune system." Richard S. Beaser MD

Many authoritative statements concur on the negative aspects of a high carb diet. We enjoy the taste of course, and the carbs provide energy, but it's an imposition on the assimilation of food. After a large carb meal the body has to deal with glucose overload. What is it going to do with it? The glucose goes into the bloodstream and circulates. Carbs raise level of blood sugar faster than protein or fat. The glycemic index helps to clarify that. Left over glucose in the bloodstream is converted to fat by insulin. With more fat in the body, body cells are less receptive to accepting insulin. (Insulin resistance = Type 2)

This is nothing less than another milestone of mine of which there has been many. Each one with a tender thought or memory that receded into a murky dim past. Hail and farewell to Carlson's Bakery and those early bird crafters that I would forget or allow to fade from memory.

Alack and alas, but that I might enjoy a tad bit on occasion and recall a niche from the past.

A niche that hosted in remembrance:

- Mom's Banana Apple Bread
- Golden Almond Fruit Cake
- Hot Pepper Gingerbread with Orange Maple Butter
- Double Dark Chocolate Cherry Cookies
- Black Bottom Brownies
- Sour Cherry and Almond Biscotti
- Chocolate Orange Macaroons
- Coconut Cake with Passion Fruit Filling
- Hazelnut Raspberry Layer Cake
- Sweet Plum Clafoutis with Almonds
- Strawberry Shortcake
- Sour Cherry Pie with Pistacchio Crumble
- Lemon Blueberry Buttermilk Pie
- Apple Orchard Pecan Crumble
- Sweet Melissa's Hot Fudge Sauce
- Lemon Blueberry Cheesecake with Cornmeal Crust
- Chocolate Raspberry Truffle Torte
- Butter Toffee Crunch

At this point I am hopeful that although something may have been lost, something may have been gained.

I would now close all books and research. I have done a major change in my diet.

This morning I tried a protein breakfast rather than oatmeal.

Egg Pancake

1 TBSP - Butter
2 - Eggs
Salt & Pepper
Sautéed Onions
Tomato Salsa
Chopped Meat (Bacon)

Melt butter, add eggs and stir. Drop on plate and add salt and pepper or some chopped veggies. I rolled it up in two whole wheat tortillas and put one wrapped in frig. It was a mouthful. Added some steamed veggies.

Not Bad. So I have done a crossover to more protein and less carbs. Would anyone wonder why I am the author of "Confessions of a Carbohydrate Addict."

15

The Cottage By The Sea

A place called home was my passion
Not so grand, but in my fashion
Simple yet, with everything
To please my soul and make me sing
From this abode to be my pleasure
The primrose path, which has no measure
With creeping vines and garden too
A wooden seat to yield a view
This humble home to draw a sigh
By one who dreamed, such as I
Who lives within, I would envy
The cottage by the sea

Down to the shore and find a trail
See startled birds and a distant sail
Just as far as eye can reach
Waves unfurled against the beach
My presence there, I left my sign
Sandy footprints, they were mine
I'll put my name upon the door
Where to live for evermore
Know that others may envy
The cottage by the sea

Tending garden, I'd be there
No better place to show I care
For flowers, creepers or a phlox
Gather for any window box
Down to the beach, where wind and surf
Try so hard to shake the earth
A quiet time invites a lull
Bear the plaintive white winged gull
In this retreat at end of day
Enjoy rapport with natures way
A quest by some who would envy
The cottage by the sea

By Ken Heckersen

About the Author

Kenneth Andrew Heckerson was born on August 31, 1919 in Hull, England. His Father was Swedish and his mother was English and Irish. He grew up with 3 older brothers and 1 younger brother.

The family moved to the United States in 1920 and settled in St Joseph, MO. His father was a sailor. The family moved to Chicago, IL in 1924 when Ken was 5 years old and he did his schooling there.

After graduation, 1942-1945, Ken enlisted in the Army and was stationed in Hawaii and Solomon Islands in the South Pacific during WWII.

After the military, Ken settled in San Francisco for 1 year. From 1946-1951, he was in Los Angeles working as a traveling salesman selling undercoating for automobiles.

Ken decided to move back to the Midwest, and from 1951-2006, he lived in Milwaukee, WI for 55 years as a property manager.

Ken officially retired in 2006 and moved to Prairie du Chien for 1 year. However, there wasn't enough action for him there so he visited La Crosse. In 2007 La Crosse became his home and he spent the last 15 years in "God's Country" enjoying every minute of his life!

SPORTS
COMICS
FINANCIAL
THE CHICAGO SUN
SECOND SECTION   MONDAY, OCTOBER 22, 1945   ★★★   PAGE 15
CLA
OBITUA

WHAT THE WELL DRESSED VETERAN WILL WEAR DEMONSTRATED TO G.I.s BY FORMER BUDDIES

recently discharged servicemen demonstrated to more than 3,000 servicemen and how to "reconvert" successfully to civilian life in co-operation with the State St. Here they are at left in uniforms. From left: Corp. Francis J. Fagan, 7893 av.; T/3 Franklin E. Householder, 509 Elmwood av., Evanston; Pvt. Robert P. Ottawa, Ill.; T/4 Kenneth Heckerson, 3049 Kenmore av.; S.Sgt. Lennard J. 6651 Washington blvd.; Yeoman 1/c John J. Lokker, Holland, Mich.; BM1/c

L. J. Forsyth, Viola, Ill.; and Sgt. Wilbert E. Goorsky, U.S. Marines, 164 av. And there they are at right dressed in what the smart civilian wears. show was staged in the old Auditorium Theater, now part of the Michigan g Center. The models were all battle-starred heroes recently discharged from or Marines. A more glamorous touch was added by pretty girls from the Room Only," who showed off the latest feminine frills.

ARMY DISCHARGE

IT TOOK ME
99
YEARS
TO LOOK THIS GOOD

0 Years of
& Regret
Let's
Par-t
Ken H.
IT TOOK ME
100
YEARS
TO LOOK THIS GOOD